It's Halloween, Dear Dragon

by Margaret Hillert
Illustrated by Carl Kock

NORWOOD HOUSE PRESS

DEAR CAREGIVER, The *Beginning-to-Read* series is a carefully written collection of classic readers you may remember from your own childhood. Each book features text comprised of common sight words to provide your child ample practice reading the words that appear most frequently in written text. The many additional details in the pictures enhance the story and offer the opportunity for you to help your child expand oral language and develop comprehension.

Begin by reading the story to your child, followed by letting him or her read familiar words and soon your child will be able to read the story independently. At each step of the way, be sure to praise your reader's efforts to build his or her confidence as an independent reader. Discuss the pictures and encourage your child to make connections between the story and his or her own life. At the end of the story, you will find reading activities and a word list that will help your child practice and strengthen beginning reading skills.

Above all, the most important part of the reading experience is to have fun and enjoy it!

Shannon Cannon

Shannon Cannon,
Literacy Consultant

Norwood House Press • P.O. Box 316598 • Chicago, Illinois 60631
For more information about Norwood House Press please visit our website at
www.norwoodhousepress.com or call 866-565-2900.

LIBRARY OF CONGRESS CATALOGING-IN-PUBLICATION DATA

Hillert, Margaret.
  It's Halloween, dear dragon / by Margaret Hillert; illustrated by
Carl Kock. — Rev. and expanded library ed.
    p. cm. — (Beginning to read series. Dear dragon)
  Summary: A boy and his pet dragon play in the autumn leaves,
  make a jack-o'-lantern, eat pumpkin pie, dress in costumes, go
  trick-or-treating, enter a costume contest, and fly together. Includes
  reading activities.
  ISBN-13: 978-1-59953-041-3 (library binding : alk. paper)
  ISBN-10: 1-59953-041-4 (library binding : alk. paper)
  [1. Halloween—Fiction. 2. Dragons—Fiction.] I. Kock, Carl, ill.
II. Title. III. Series.
PZ7.H558It 2007
[E]—dc22   2006007087

Beginning-to-Read series (c) 2007 by Margaret Hillert.
Library edition published by permission of Pearson Education, Inc. in
arrangement with Norwood House Press, Inc. All rights reserved.
This book was originally published by Follett Publishing Company in 1981.

Look up here.
Do you see what I see?
Something red.
Something yellow.

And look down here.
We can play here.
This is fun.

5

See what I can do.
I can make you look funny.
Oh, oh, oh.
Funny, funny you.

I can work, too.
Work, work, work.
I can help Father.

7

Come here. Come here.
You can work, too.
You can help do this.

8

Now come with me.
I want to get something.
You can help.
Run, run, run.

Here is a big one.
We want this one.
And a little one, too.

Father, Father.
Look what we have.
Can you help us make something?

I can. I can.
I can do it.
Look at this.
Do you like this?

And look at this one.
I can make it funny.
It looks like you.

Here, little one.
Come up here.
This is something funny.
Do you want to see this?

Mother, Mother.
Can you make something, too?
Can you make something for us?

Yes, I can.
I can make something good.
You will like it.

Look at me.
See what I have.
Guess who I am.
Guess, guess.

We will get something here.
Something good.
We can eat it.
This is fun.

Not you.
Not you.
No, you will not do.

Here.
You are the one.
Here is something for you.
You are funny.

Oh, my.
What do I see?
What do you have here?

Look what we can do.
Away we go.
Up, up, and away!
What a good ride.

Here you are with me.
And here I am with you.
Oh, what a happy Halloween, dear dragon.

The following activities support the findings of the National Reading Panel that determined the most effective components for reading instruction are: Phonemic Awareness, Phonics, Vocabulary, Fluency, and Text Comprehension.

Phonemic Awareness: The /h/ sound

Sound Substitution: Say the words on the left to your child. Ask your child to repeat the word, changing the first sound to /**h**/:

pot = hot	book = hook	seal = heal	pat = hat
card = hard	sit = hit	ball = hall	top = hop
nose = hose	tip = hip	jam = ham	seat = heat

Phonics: The letter Hh

1. Demonstrate how to form the letters **H** and **h** for your child.

2. Have your child practice writing **H** and **h** at least three times each.

3. Ask your child to point to the words in the book that begin with the letter **h**.

4. Write down the following words and ask your child to write the letter **h** in front of them to make a new word:

__air	__and	__eat	__old
__eel	__ear	__is	__ill

5. Read the words aloud. Ask your child to read all the words he or she knows.

Vocabulary: Contractions

1. Explain to your child that sometimes we combine two words to make one shorter word and that these new words are called contractions.

2. Point to the word It's on the front cover. Ask your child to name the two

words that make It's. If your child doesn't know, explain that the word It's comes from the two words it and is.

3. Say the following contractions and ask your child to name the words that make each one:

| don't | she's | can't | he'll | we've |
| I'll | doesn't | you're | isn't | they're |

4. Write the following contractions and word pairs on separate pieces of paper.

did not / didn't	we will / we'll	are not / aren't
was not / wasn't	that is / that's	I am / I'm
we are / we're	you will / you'll	did not / didn't
you are / you're	let us / let's	it will / it'll

5. Ask your child to match the word pairs with the contractions they make.

Fluency: Shared Reading

1. Reread the story to your child at least two more times while your child tracks the print by running a finger under the words as they are read. Ask your child to read the words he or she knows with you.

2. Reread the story taking turns, alternating readers between sentences or pages.

Text Comprehension: Discussion Time

1. Ask your child to retell the sequence of events in the story.

2. To check comprehension, ask your child the following questions:

   • How did the boy and Dear Dragon help Father?

   • What did Mother and Father do with the pumpkins?

   • How did the boy make the jack-o-lantern look like Dear Dragon?

   • Which parts of the story could really happen? Which parts are make believe?

   • What do you do to celebrate Halloween?

WORD LIST

It's Halloween, Dear Dragon uses the 64 words listed below.
This list can be used to practice reading the words that appear in the text. You may wish to write the words on index cards and use them to help your child build automatic word recognition. Regular practice with these words will enhance your child's fluency in reading connected text.

a	father	like	red	want
am	for	little	ride	we
and	fun	look(s)	run	what
are	funny			who
at		make	see	will
away	get	me	something	with
	go	mother		work
big	good	my	the	
	guess		this	yellow
can		no	to	yes
come	Halloween	not	too	you
	happy	now		
dear	have		up	
do	help	oh	us	
down	here	one		
dragon				
	I	play		
eat	is			
	it ('s)			

ABOUT THE AUTHOR Margaret Hillert has written over 80 books for children who are just learning to read. Her books have been translated into many different languages and over a million children throughout the world have read her books. She first started writing poetry as a child and has continued to write for children and adults throughout her life. A first grade teacher for 34 years, Margaret is now retired from teaching and lives in Michigan where she likes to write, take walks in the morning, and care for her three cats.

Photograph by Glenna Washburn

ABOUT THE ADVISER Shannon Cannon contributed the activities pages that appear in this book. Shannon serves as a literacy consultant and provides staff development to help improve reading instruction. She is a frequent presenter at educational conferences and workshops. Prior to this she worked as an elementary school teacher and as president of a curriculum publishing company.